LOCKDOWN HORROR #3

Compiled & Edited by

Ben Thomas | D. Kershaw | S.N. Graves

Also available and coming soon
from Black Hare Press

DARK DRABBLES ANTHOLOGIES

WORLDS	APOCALYPSE
ANGELS	LOVE
MONSTERS	HATE
BEYOND	OCEANS
UNRAVEL	ANCIENTS

BHP WRITERS' GROUP SPECIAL EDITIONS

STORMING AREA 51	BAD ROMANCE
EERIE CHRISTMAS	TWENTY TWENTY

OTHER VOLUMES

DEEP SPACE	DEEP SEA
WHAT IF?	BEYOND THE REALM
KEY TO THE KINGDOM	

Twitter: @BlackHarePress
Facebook: BlackHarePress
Website: www.BlackHarePress.com

Cover design	Dawn Burdett	www.dmburdett.com
Formatting	Ben Thomas	www.blackharepress.com
Editing	D. Kershaw	www.blackharepress.com
	S.N. Graves	www.sngraves.com
Read Team	David Green	davidgreenwritercom.wordpress.com
	Jennifer Hatfield	jhatfieldauthor.wixsite.com/website
	Jodi Jensen	jodijensenwrites.wordpress.com
	Lyndsay Ellis-Holloway	authorlyndseyellisholloway.webador.co.uk
	Maggie Pawsey	
	Stacey Jaine McIntosh	www.staceyjainemcintosh.com

TABLE OF CONTENTS

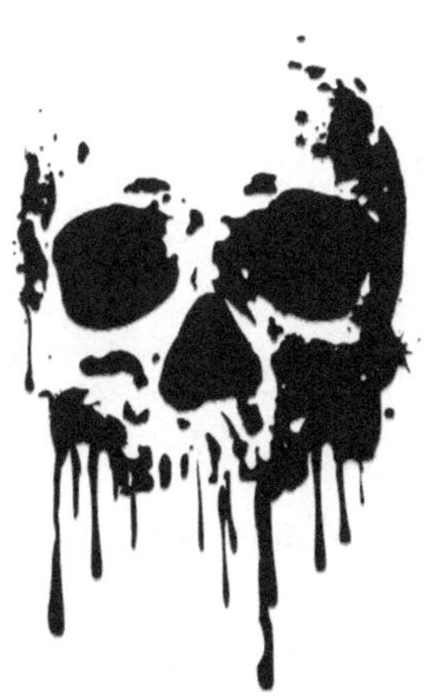

THEY SAY CROWS CAN REMEMBER FACES

By Warren Benedetto

The stone hit Ava in the back of the head. She stumbled and fell, spilling her schoolbooks out of her arms and onto the dirt road in front of her. Her hands flew out to break her fall. Gravel dug into her palms. Her knees skidded painfully across the ground.

"Have a nice trip!" a boy's voice behind her called out, to a chorus of laughter. "See you next fall!"

Ava brushed her long, black hair out of her face. She was hollow-boned and delicate, looking far younger than her 11 years. Her dark eyes welled with tears. She quickly wiped them away with the frayed cuff of her sweater.

A chilly autumn wind blew across the Kansas field. Corn stalks whispered in the breeze. Somewhere in the distance, a gas-powered tractor growled. The sound was faint and far. It was probably from

Mr Conklin's farm—he was the only farmer in the area who was wealthy enough to own a tractor—but it didn't matter. He wasn't close enough to help her. Nobody was. She was alone.

A group of kids about her age, two girls and a boy, ran past her. One of the girls stuck out her tongue. The other one laughed. Their shoes kicked up clouds of dust into Ava's face as they passed.

The girls were sisters, Sarah and Beth Winters. They were pretty and clean, with crisp, red bows tied in their flaxen hair. They were the kinds of girls who had everything they needed and got everything they wanted; they never had to ask for anything twice. They wore matching blue dresses with warm red sweaters that looked like they were bought from a department store. Not handmade, like Ava's shapeless brown smock. They weren't twins—Sarah was two years older than Beth—but they were inseparable. Even now, they held hands as they skipped away into the distance. Ava hated them both. Equally.

The boy was Carl. He must have had a last name, but Ava didn't know it. It didn't matter. There was only one Carl. He was a lumbering giant, easily a foot taller than anyone else in the class, with an oversized head that reminded Ava of a rotten pumpkin. His belly hung over his belt, straining the buttons of his denim shirt. His ruddy cheeks were sunburned and freckled from a long summer of torturing rabbits and stoning squirrels. He had icy blue-grey eyes, the colour of the sky before a winter storm. He was stupid and mean and cruel. Not in that order.

Ava touched her fingers to the back of her head, where the stone had hit her. It wasn't a big stone, but it was angular and sharp. She drew her fingers away. They were slick with blood. Not a lot—the wound would scab up just fine—but enough to bring on a fresh swell of tears. She swallowed hard, choking back a sob. *No,* she thought. *No crying. Not this time.*

She was angry. At them, yes, but also at herself. She should have heard them coming. She was off in her own world again, like an idiot. She should have known they were behind her. They usually were. Sometimes they left her alone, if she was far enough ahead of them. But if she was in range—throwing distance or shouting distance, depending on the day—they were pretty consistently awful. Especially Carl.

In the winter, he threw snowballs. The rest of the year, it was rocks. Or rotten fruit. Or worse. A few weeks ago, he threw a dead rat. He found it on the side of the road, picked it up by the tail, and slung it at Ava as he passed. It slapped her on the side of the face, exploding in a putrescent eruption of maggot-infested entrails. The squirming, blood-blackened mass slid down her face and onto her shoulder, then rolled down her back to the ground. Ava gagged at the smell, hot vomit spilling from her lips and down the front of her dress.

Compared to that, Ava preferred the

rocks. They hurt more, but at least she didn't have to spend the rest of the day stinking of puke and decay.

Ava picked herself up off the ground, brushed the dirt and gravel from her scraped knees, and gathered up her books. She would be late for school today, for sure. And Mrs Harrison would be angry, as usual. Ava would try to explain, but Mrs Harrison would hear none of it. She would put Ava in the corner at the front of the room, alone, facing the rest of the class, under the painting of Jesus and the apostles. The "prayer corner," she called it, where she expected—commanded—that Ava pray for forgiveness.

Ava never did.

The other kids would stare at her.

Making faces, exchanging whispers. She would look at her papers, at her hands, at the ceiling. At anything but her classmates and their horrible, hateful eyes. Mocking her. Judging her. Pitying her.

Poor Ava, in her handmade dress and second-hand shoes. Poor Ava, whose father was a drunk and whose mother was a cripple. Poor Ava, who had no money and no friends. Poor, poor Ava.

They were right. She was poor. But she had one thing that none of them had.

A secret.

***

"Look, she's doing it again," Carl said. He took a huge bite of a sandwich, his third.

It was lunchtime. The students were out on the playground behind their one-room schoolhouse, playing on wooden equipment hand-crafted by the church's Men's Club during a series of sweat-soaked, prayer-fuelled summer Saturdays. There were swings, some seesaws, a metal slide, and various other play structures.

Carl sat atop a large wooden climbing wall made from stacked logs. Sarah and Beth sat on either side of him, swinging their legs. Other children of various ages were clustered in small groups around the yard, playing jacks, jumping rope, swinging, and seesawing. Everyone except Ava. She was alone, in the corner of the playground by the edge of the woods, staring up into a tree. Talking.

"She's so weird," Sarah stage-whispered.

Beth squinted, shielding her eyes against the glare of the sun. "Who's she talking to?"

"Not who. What," Sarah corrected.

Carl pointed one thick-knuckled finger. "In the tree," he said through a mouthful of food. "See the crow?"

Sure enough, a large crow was perched on the branch above Ava's head. It looked down at her, head cocked to the side, listening. Ava pulled a small piece of bread from the slice in her hand and tossed it up to the bird. The crow caught it in mid-air and gulped it down greedily.

"Maybe it knows her," Beth offered. She leaned out so she could see Sarah around Carl's considerable bulk. "Like Uncle Jeff's, remember?"

"Right, it knows her," Carl replied sarcastically.

Sarah nodded in agreement with Beth. "Could be. Crows can remember faces. Our mom said so."

"Uncle Jeff used to always feed the same crow whenever he came over to our house," Beth added. "He'd get out of his truck, and a minute later, this huge, black crow would swoop down, right to his shoulder, looking for bread. He used to keep a slice in his shirt pocket, just for that."

"Probably wasn't the same one," Carl mumbled, waving his hand dismissively.

"Sure was!" Beth said, defensive.

"How many people you know have a crow land on their shoulder?"

"Okay, then." Carl lifted his sandwich into the air in a mock salute. "To Uncle Jeff," he proclaimed. "World's Worst Scarecrow." He took another big bite of his sandwich.

Beth punched him playfully in the arm, laughing. "*You're* the worst!"

Carl finished chewing. He licked his fingers clean, then wiped them on his pants. His expression turned serious. He nodded towards Ava. She was still looking up into the tree, talking to the crow. "You know what I think?" he asked. "I think she's a witch. Like her mom."

"Her mom's a witch?" Beth asked, surprised. She shot a questioning look at

Sarah to confirm.

Sarah rolled her eyes. "Oh, great. This again," she scoffed.

"Everybody knows it," Carl insisted. "Ask my dad. Remember a few years ago, when all our sheep died?"

"You said wolves did that," Sarah reminded him.

"Their eyes were ripped out!" Carl exclaimed. Beth grimaced. "Wolves don't do that. Not normal ones, anyway."

"What does, then?" Beth asked, wide-eyed. She was hanging on Carl's every word.

Sarah whispered to Carl, just out of Beth's earshot. "Stop. You're scaring her."

Carl ignored Sarah, instead explaining to Beth, "Witches talk to animals, tell them to do things, use them to get back at people. That's what her mom did."

"But why?" Beth asked.

"My dad says she's jealous. She used to be sweet on him. Still is, he says."

"If Ava's a witch, then why doesn't she look like one?" Sarah asked, challenging him.

"She doesn't need to," Carl insisted. "Real witches look normal, just like us."

"Maybe he's right," Beth said. "Maybe she is." Her voice was full of awe.

Sarah kicked at Carl. "Great, now she believes you." She shook her head. "She's not," Sarah said to Beth. "He's just joshing you. There's no such thing."

"No?" Carl jumped down from the climbing wall, landing with a thud. "Okay, let's ask her."

"Carl, don't—" Sarah began, but Carl was already loping over to Ava. He thrust his hands deep in pockets, trying to project an aura of innocent curiosity.

"Hey, Ava," he called. "Whatcha doing?"

Ava froze. She quickly averted her eyes away from the crow, casting them downwards. She toed the ground with one foot but didn't turn around. "Nothing," she said quietly.

"Can you help us with something?" Carl asked, his voice honey-sweet. "Sarah and Beth and me?" He motioned towards the sisters, who were still perched on top of the climbing wall. Sarah beckoned to Carl to come back. He shook his head.

Ava didn't respond, so Carl continued. "That bird up there." He nodded towards the crow still perched on the branch overhead. It peered down at them with focused attention, as if eavesdropping on their conversation. "Were you just talking to it?"

Still no response from Ava. Carl put his hands on his knees and leaned in close to Ava's face, trying to look her in the eye. "What are you two talking about, huh?"

Ava's lips moved imperceptibly; her voice barely audible.

Carl cupped his hand to his ear and raised his voice. "What's that? Couldn't hear you."

"He's my friend," Ava said, slightly louder this time.

"Your friend?" Carl said, incredulous. He laughed loudly, slapping his knee. Ava flinched at the sound. "Your only one, I'll bet."

Ava didn't answer.

"Does he talk back?" Carl continued. He leaned in closer, leering. Taunting. "What does he say? Does he tell you he likes you? Does he tell you you're pretty?"

Ava's cheeks flushed. Hot crimson patches spread across her chest and up her neck.

"Hey, you know who talks to animals?" Carl said brightly, as if the idea just occurred to him. "Witches." He lowered his voice and whispered conspiratorially. "You're not a witch, are you?"

Ava shook her head slowly.

"How about your mom? Is *she* a witch?"

Ava shook her head again.

"You're sure? I won't tell."

Ava nodded.

"Okay, good. Just wanted to check." Carl straightened up, cracked his neck, then started to back away. Ava seemed to relax. She glanced up at the bird.

Suddenly, Carl cupped his hands around his mouth and shouted across the playground. "Hey, everyone! It's okay! Ava said she's not a witch! Her mom too! Also not a witch!"

Other kids on the playground looked towards them, wondering what the shouting was about. Some snickered amongst themselves. Others pointed at Ava and laughed. Ava bowed her head, allowing her hair to fall over her face, shielding her from their stares.

"They're just friends, is all," Carl yelled. "Ava and the crow! Best friends!"

"Carl, stop," Sarah called. "Leave her alone."

Carl walked back over towards the climbing wall, a grin on his face. "You're such a spoil-sport," he said to Sarah.

Sarah raised her chin and looked away. "It's just not funny, that's all."

Carl glanced back over at Ava. She was now sitting on the ground, hugging her knees to her chest, staring at her shoes. The crow glided down from the tree and landed at her feet. It pecked the dirt around her, picking up stray breadcrumbs.

"Watch this," Carl said. He reached down and scooped a rock from the playground sand. It was heavy and round, about the size of a golf ball.

"Don't!" Sarah hissed. "You're going to get us in trouble!"

Carl snorted derisively. He gripped the rock like a split-finger fastball, then whipped it sidearm towards Ava. The rock sliced through the air with deadly precision and caught the crow square in the side of its head, instantly shattering its delicate skull and rupturing its eye. Ava recoiled backwards, shocked by the sudden violence of the impact. The crow flopped over on its side. One of its wings extended at a crooked angle and gave a single weak flap.

Carl pumped his fist in excitement. "Yes! Direct hit!"

When Ava recovered enough to realise what happened, she let out an agonising cry. "Nooooooo!" she screamed. "No, no, no!"

She gathered up the broken bird in her arms and cradled it on its back, like a mother holding a newborn. The crow's head rotated loosely and grotesquely on its broken neck. Ava slipped her palm under its head, supporting it.

Carl stepped closer, looking down over Ava's shoulder at the dying bird. Its skull was split wide open, crimson-flecked white bone standing out in stark contrast to the black feathers. Thick ropes of blood and gore oozed from the wound, mixing with the clear fluid leaking from its destroyed eye. The crow looked up at Ava with its one good eye. It blinked once, its pupil turning white, then black again. Its beak opened and closed silently a few times, then stopped. It was dead.

Sarah started climbing down from her perch on the wall. "C'mon, Beth," she said, tugging her sister's hem. "Before we get in trouble." Beth followed her sister to the ground. Sarah regarded Carl with disgust. "You didn't have to do that. It wasn't hurting anyone."

"Oh, stop!" he exclaimed. "What's the big deal? It's just a bird!"

Sarah grabbed her younger sister's hand and pulled her towards the schoolhouse. "Let's go."

"Really?" Carl called after them. "You guys! C'mon, you guys!"

They ignored him and walked hand-in-hand into the school. Carl looked down at Ava. She was hugging the bird's lifeless body to her chest, rocking it slowly and whispering to it.

"Burn in hell, witch," Carl sneered. Then, he ran off to catch up with Sarah and Beth.

Ava didn't acknowledge him. Her eyes were fixed on a second crow, high overhead, silhouetted against the afternoon sun as it circled over the playground. Watching.

***

After class, Carl changed from his school clothes to his regular at-home attire: a pair of denim overalls over a dingy white t-shirt, and a pair of square-toed black boots with heavy rubber soles.

He had chores to do. School was back in session, which meant winter was only a few short weeks away. Already, the days were getting shorter, and the sun was setting earlier. The nights were chilly. Soon they would be freezing, and his father would need to heat up the wood stove to keep their small house warm.

It was up to Carl to ensure they had enough firewood to make it through the season. That meant spending long hours splitting logs and stacking the wood in the shed behind the house, where it would stay dry until it was needed. It was hard work, but Carl found comfort in it. He liked the weight of the axe, the way it arced through the air and split the logs so easily. It made him feel strong.

Carl's house was nestled back in the woods, a hundred yards or more from the road. It was a tiny three-room shack with leaded windows and a rusted tin roof, hand-built by his father from trees he felled in the forest. A small stream trickled nearby. Occasionally, Carl would fish in the stream, but mostly he just pissed in it. When nobody was looking, of course.

Nobody was looking now, so Carl embedded his axe in the chopping block, ambled over to the stream, unzipped his fly, and directed a spray of urine into the slow-moving water. He whistled tunelessly. His eyes wandered across the trees on the waterline until they settled on a thick branch that extended from a large, crooked oak on the other side of the stream. Sitting on the branch was a large crow. It ruffled its feathers, then peered down at Carl.

"What?" Carl sneered. "You want this?" He moved his hips in a circle, pissing a ring into the water.

"Caw!" the crow said. Then, with incredible quickness, it launched itself off the branch and swooped directly at Carl's head.

Carl ducked sideways, gasping in surprise. His boots squelched in the soft mud of the stream bank. He lost his balance and fell hard, smacking his tailbone on the rocks embedded in the dirt. His head hit the ground with a dull thud. A cry of pain and shock spit from his lips.

"Goddamn it!" he cursed. "What the hell?"

Mumbling under his breath, he sat up and rubbed his hand across the back of his head. No blood, thank God. He brushed the dirt and leaves out of his hair, then scanned the trees overhead for the bird. It was gone.

He pulled himself to his feet, zipped his fly, then surveyed the damage. His overalls were soaked up the back with foul-smelling mud, from his ankles to his asshole. More mud was smeared across the backs of both arms. His boots were water-logged. *Great,* he thought. *Now I'm in for it.* If his father saw what a mess he was, he'd tan Carl's hide for sure.

Carl trudged across the yard, unbuckling his overalls as he went. He'd need to strip down, rinse his clothes in the pump from the well, then hang them on the line to dry. Carl sat down on the chopping block, unlaced his boots, and tugged them off his feet. Then he peeled off the heavy, mud-soaked denim, dropping it in a wet pile on the ground. He retrieved a wooden bucket from a rusty hook on the side of the woodshed, gathered his overalls in the bucket, then carried it over to the black iron water pump nearby.

He started working the pump handle. After a minute or so, water began to trickle—then pour—from the curved metal mouth of the pump's spout. Carl ran one arm under the water, then the other, rinsing away the now-dry mud. Then he cupped some water into his mouth and splashed some on his face. The water was ice cold, with a coppery metallic tinge that reminded him of how a bloody lip tasted. He patted his face dry on his t-shirt, then opened his eyes.

Mere inches away, a crow was perched on the water pump, studying him. It was eerily still. Focused.

"Jesus!" Carl cursed, startled.

He swatted at the crow. The bird hopped backwards down the pump handle and flapped its wings to maintain its balance, but it did not flee. If anything, it seemed even less afraid.

"Get out of here!" Carl shouted.

The bird just glared at him, its coal-black eyes sparkling with fearless defiance.

"Caw!" it called out. In an instant, three more crows descended from a nearby tree, landing on the ground a few feet in front of Carl.

"Fuck off!" Carl yelled. "Leave me alone!" He kicked at the wooden bucket, knocking it over in their direction. His soaking overalls tumbled out of the bucket onto the ground. A flood of water rolled towards the birds. They calmly lifted into the air until it passed, then settled back down on the sodden grass. Then they, too, began to call.

"Caw! Caw! Caw!"

Several more crows called out in response. Within seconds, the three on the ground were joined by five more. Then ten. Then twenty. The calls grew louder as their numbers multiplied, in turn drawing even more. Some emerged from the woods; others materialised on the horizon, silhouetted against the fading afternoon light. They perched all around Carl: high and low, on trees and on the ground, on the roof of the house and on the woodshed. All of them calling, their cries overlapping.

As they multiplied, their calls started to morph into something different. It didn't sound like they were screaming "Caw!" anymore.

It sounded like they were screaming "Carl."

Carl looked around wildly. The crows were closing in from all sides, a maelstrom of shadows swooping and circling in ever-tighter formation around him. They blotted out the sky above, leaving nothing visible overhead but a roiling ocean of black feathers. Carl picked up the wooden bucket and hurled it at the birds in front of him. The crows in its path dipped and swerved to avoid the projectile, then quickly reassembled in the same formation. Circling him closer. And closer.

The crow on the water pump was the first to strike. It launched itself like a rifle shot aimed right at Carl's head. Carl threw up his arms to shield his face. The crow's beak struck his forearm, carving a thick slice through the freckled flesh. Fresh blood surged from the wound.

Carl turned to run, but he found his

path blocked by still more crows. He kicked and swung at them, feeling his hands and arms connecting with their bodies, their hollow bones collapsing on impact. But there were too many. Their beaks tore at his arms. His legs. His torso. Others launched themselves at his head. At his face.

Carl stumbled backwards. His feet tangled in the soaking overalls on the ground, twisting his leg at an unnatural angle. As he fell, his shin bone snapped with a sickening crack loud enough to be heard even above the din of the crows' calls. The splintered end of the broken bone tore through his skin. He hit the ground hard, fracturing his ribs and knocking the wind from his lungs. He gasped for air.

Clutched at his leg. And screamed.

Then, the crows were upon him.

***

Ava lay on the cot in her bedroom, listening. In the distance, she could hear the cries of dozens of crows. Hundreds, maybe. And something else, almost lost in the cacophony. Screams.

Suddenly, there was a tapping on her window. Ava sat up and swung her feet to the floor, the cot springs squeaking with relief as she stood. She glided across the room. Peered through the dusty glass. And smiled.

There, on the roof outside the window, was a crow. It held something round and white in its beak.

An eye.

Ava opened the window. The crow placed the eye delicately on the windowsill, then stepped backwards. The eye rolled towards Ava. She picked it up and examined it in her palm. The orb was greyish-white, with fine red blood vessels spidering throughout. The short stub of the severed optic stalk protruded from the back. The iris of the eye was an icy blue-grey, the colour of the sky before a winter storm.

"Thank you," Ava said to the crow.

The crow blinked, then bowed its head, inviting Ava to pet it. Ava reached out and gently ruffled the feathers on the back of the bird's neck.

"Now," she continued. "Bring me the other."

ASHES TO ASHES

By Jasmine Jarvis

There sits a house on an abandoned farm. Broken fences mark out the paddock perimeters; grass and weeds as high as your waist cover the ground once worn down by cattle and sheep. The dirt drive leading up to the timber farmhouse is littered with potholes and divots; you don't dare drive your car as it will break the suspension. You go by foot. The crunching of the dirt underneath your feet sounds louder than normal, or perhaps it is because out here it is too quiet? No bird song, no wind. The trees dotted throughout the paddocks slouch under the weight of their branches, full of lush green leaves. The weeds ripple like the water's surface, caressed by a breeze—a breeze that you yourself cannot feel.

You tug at a long strand of grass and begin to wave it about as you walk up along the drive. The sun is warm, and you begin to feel beads of sweat tickle your back. You turn your attention to the wooden bones that were once shelters for the cattle, a place for them to huddle under to escape the elements. Now they are nothing more than blackened, jagged beams jutting up through the weeds. The tin sheets that were once the roofing, rusted through and propped up against the wooden skeletons. The weeds ripple, and you stop. You hold your arms out in front of you, watching the bare skin, but you feel nothing. You physically do not respond to the wind. Is it even there? The long blade of grass in your fingertips gently bobs and sways, but the hairs on your arms remain motionless. Not a single goose bump. You move on towards the house, leaping over potholes; some are filled with water following the summer shower that came over in the morning.

Crunch, crunch, crunch.

So loud in such a quiet place. Will you get caught out for making so much noise? Don't be silly! There is no one here but you. The farm has been abandoned for over thirty years and though you can't remember what caused the people to leave, you can feel it. That *something*. Like a fire in your brain. Rivulets of sweat are now racing down your back and you squirm as you walk. You reach behind you and tug at your T-shirt to let air flow up and onto your back to try to dry you out. Your armpits begin to feel wet, and you wipe sweat from your brow. The humidity is starting to peak after the rain this morning. Why would you want to come here during the hottest time of the year? You had always seen this place in your dreams. Always from the outside though, your dreams never allowed you to venture inside it, stopping as you would walk inside. From what you did see, you were struck with a sense of familiarity. Until today, you never thought that this place really existed. Driving interstate, moving to a new job, you caught sight of it as you wound along the backroads of the middle of nowhere—the house sitting up on its little hill—and you stopped your car, leaving it by the side of the road; you began to make your way to the place that you feel had been such a big part of your life, but what exactly that part was, you are not entirely sure.

Crunch, crunch, crunch.

The silence was surreal. The moment your feet crossed over the threshold of that driveway, all noise stopped.

Crunch, crunch, crunch.

Closer to the barn now, rounding up towards the house. The barn, with its doors long gone, inside it, it is dark. The once red coat is now blistered and peeling. In some parts it has been completely stripped by the elements. The pulley swings slowly from side to side from the top of the barn where they would have used it to hoist the sacks of grain up to the top for storage. The pulley is rusted, and despite rocking from side to side in the breeze, it makes no sound. As you walk by the front of the barn, you peer into the dark. In the dimness you can make out some stalls, but other than that the place is bare. It feels cooler standing here in the doorway, and you savour it for a moment before returning to the purpose of your visit, to go into the house.

You strike out at the stones, kicking them as you reach the porch of the house. It is as you have always seen it in your mind. Paint long gone, and the timber is grey and rough. Splinters of wood poke out, and you step up each step slowly, one boot after the other. The stairs shift, but make no noise as you go up one, two, three, four, to come to stand on the porch. It runs the entire length of the front of the house. Chains dangle from where a love seat had once been hung. Broken pots and planter tubs are scattered along the front of the porch; the flowers once tended to by the farmer's wife long gone, dust like everything else. Crossing the grey porch, you reach out to open the screen door. Fresh air is replaced with a damp, musty smell as you step inside. You sneeze and clear your throat. The front wooden door sits inside the entry, propped against the cloakroom door. Its hinges twisted and buckled—the door had been wrenched from the hinges with force.

***

Steps fall silently as you walk further inside. The crunch of your boots up the driveway is now replaced by the air moving in and out of your lungs. Slow and steady are your breaths; you have nothing to fear. The place is empty. Wallpaper hangs down in strips—pieces that remained tacked to the wall have black mould covering the once floral prints picked out by the farmer's wife. Frames lay broken along the skirting boards, their strings and hooks that once held them to the walls disintegrated long ago. The photos within are so damaged it is hard to make out the family, but if you squint and hold it up to the light in a certain way you can just make out the image of the farmer, his wife, and their three children. You let the photo fall from your hand, and it flutters back to the pile of shattered glass and broken frames. The front room, the family room, is lit by the glow of the midday sun. The lace curtains are now tendrils, lank, their tips skimming the bare wooden floor. You can see the stubs of nails which once held carpet in place. Some of them still clutch the remnants of threads. You don't walk into the little room. Instead from the doorway you take in the scene—a cane rocking chair, a little two-seater sofa. In between is an old radio. On the other side of the room an old television set—a black and white one, its antennas still upright, searching for a signal. On the small stand is a pile of books, and there appears to be some sort of staining on them. You notice that there are some dark patches on the fabric of the sofa and the cushions on the rocking chair. Mould, or…blood?

You step back into the hallway, and

you look down towards the kitchen. The light streaming in through the windows down there is flickering. You are drawn to it. Noiselessly you move along the hall, passing the stands of faded photographs, moulded envelopes that hold bills and letters from long ago. Not a sound as you reach the kitchen; it is glowing amber like in the sun. The wide kitchen window lets in the light; the flickering is from the large oak tree outside, from which a tyre swing and the remains of a cubby house still cling to the branches. Through the window you watch the tyre slowly sway around in circles in the breeze; you smile to yourself.

The Pandora's Box within you begins to open.

There had been good times.

Dust coats the metal sink and bench tops. Cupboard doors slouch on their hinges; some of them are open, the little metal clasp that would lock the door in place missing. Old glassware and a few pieces of crockery and cookware is all that remains now. The Formica kitchen table in the centre, in its heyday, was a mint green, but is now bleached white from the sun's rays. The matching seats—the vinyl is cracked and faded, and yellow stuffing pokes out from the splits. The metal is tarnished. Through the dust, you can make out rings—stains from cups placed down without a coaster. You trace your finger around one of the rings, etching it in the dust. The back door is locked, but you know on the other side is the dog's kennel.

Bean was a goofy Golden Retriever, a birthday gift and the best dog anyone could wish for. You will go outside later to visit the kennel, you tell yourself, turning and leaving the kitchen to go upstairs.

Back down the hall, you stop. You can feel the hairs on the back of your neck stand up and the atmosphere start to cool down. You are no longer hot and sweaty. You look over your shoulder back to the kitchen and see the sun is still shining brightly. You go past the family room and proceed upstairs. You don't see them in the family room, standing there, a dark shadow of two adults and two children who are watching you.

After all this time, you have come home.

The stairs bow and sag in places, well worn by a family running up and down them. Threadbare carpet-the musty smell is stronger upstairs. You glance along the landing; all the bedroom doors are closed. There are three bedrooms and a bathroom. You approach the first room on the right, gently turning the knob and pushing the door open. It is the parents' room, a big bed up against one wall, wallpaper curling down and resting upon the yellowed pillows. The duvet is pale pink and stained with patches of black mould and grime. You can see the ceiling has a leak, with mould spreading out from the moist patch to cover half of the ceiling. The wooden chest of drawers is warped, the varnish bubbling and splitting. The drawers are swollen shut, making it impossible for you to look inside them. The closet is empty save for some coat hangers.

On a bedside table is a photo in a rose-coloured frame. This photo is clearer. In it is the farmer, his wife, their teenage daughter and two young sons. The sons are grinning, freckled faced, blonde-haired and dressed in matching red shirts and jeans. The teenage girl is smiling for the camera, long blonde hair, a paisley dress, and little Mary Jane shoes with knee-high socks. Ma was cuddled into Pa... Ma... Pa... Why did you think that? How odd! Your hand trembles and you put the photo back down on the bedside table. You have had enough of this room, maybe you should go and check out the other rooms. The next bedroom is the boys' bedroom—the twins. Their beds separated by a bedside table; the nightlight, a rocket ship, sits on a doily. Toys are on the floor and the toy box is open. Sunlight fills their room, and if you close your eyes, you can almost hear them laughing as they play. A weight pulls at your heart as you stand there in that space. In their space. Wallpaper, now grey, was once splashes of blue, yellow, white, red— stars and planets and rocket ships zooming through space. Above their beds were mobiles of planets. They knew all there was to know about outer space, those two boys. They didn't want to stay on the farm; they had bigger plans—just like you did. They wanted to be astronauts when they grew up. You don't want to stay here anymore. Other memories are beginning to creep in, and you are realising that you have made a mistake. You leave the room. The boys are sitting on their beds now, watching you. Soon you will see them.

The last bedroom. Her room. You approach and it feels like your skull is about to crack open—that part of your mind you had closed off so long ago, is now pushing back. Contained within the Pandora's Box is all the sorrow, the pain, the nightmare you had thought you could keep restrained. You should have kept driving. This place doesn't exist. You should not have come back. But you did. When she was younger, it was a bright and happy room, filled with soft toys and princess dolls. A rocking horse in the corner. Pink and white everywhere and on everything. It had to be pretty for their princess. Now though, the room is devoid of all colour. The bed had been burned. The curtains. You move across the room and part the curtains to let the light in and you want to cry. You wanted to come back and see the princess room, the princess room you had held onto in your memories. Not this space. Not how you last left it. There are gouges in the wall above the head of the bed. Gouges from a knife thrusted in anger at not being allowed to have what she wanted. The princess didn't like being told no. Her new friend told her she deserved so much better, and if she ran away with him, he could show her what she was missing out on. Come. Join his family.

Join his family.

You reach under the pillow and pull out two straw figures. Ma and Pa. Your hands begin to sting, and you drop them onto the burnt mattress. *He* had given them to her and told her that if her parents wouldn't let her go, she was to burn the dolls and the parents would feel it and be in agony. You remember trying to burn the dolls after Ma and Pa had told you that you were too young to leave the home. You held the flame to them but changed your mind as they began to light, quickly dropping them onto the bed, accidentally burning the mattress in the process. You had decided to forget the dolls and to try something else instead, something you had read in a book borrowed from one of your new friends, the new friends your parents didn't like. Your eyes turn to the pentagram you had carved into the wooden floorboards and you feel sick, the claws of a headache slowly sinking into your brain.

Pandora's Box is opening.

***

Now is the time to leave. Something is gnawing at you, something is about to happen like it did all those years ago, and now you must leave the house. Once out on the landing the air smells like flowers, the wallpaper is bright, floral prints. Ma had chosen the print for the house when she and Pa were building it. The hall stand has a vase of fresh flowers that Ma had picked that afternoon from the garden. The carpet was plush and dark blue again. Downstairs you can hear them talking about you. You are too young. It is just a schoolgirl crush. Pa will go and speak to this boy and his parents in the morning. Maybe they should look at another school for you? This year you have fallen in with the wrong crowd. Kids these days are so impressionable. Maybe a chat with the pastor might help? The voices of Ma and Pa travel upstairs. Behind you the twins burst from their room, racing down the stairs, flying their rocket ships. Ma yells that they are meant to be getting ready for bed, however they don't listen to her, and they continue to chase each other, finally deciding to listen to Ma when Pa brings out the belt and threatens them with it.

You stand there and watch them run up the stairs towards you; they lock eyes with you and they smile. "Outta our way, Maisie!" they holler at you, bumping you into the stair balustrade as they run into the bathroom. This isn't real, you tell yourself as you go downstairs, heading for the front door. This is all in your head. Memories. You can leave now, and when you get home, you can see a doctor to help you put the memories back into the box. Just like last time. You don't look at the photos hanging on the wall as you walk down the stairs. They are still talking in the kitchen. You just need to open that front door, and all of this will stop. You tell yourself that, but you know what is coming for them.

Maybe when you open that front door it cuts the memory off, stops the nightmare from taking them again.

Stops them from suffering again.

Your chest heaves; silent sobs punch away at you as you move through the home you once knew. You don't want to look back to see your parents. It was hard leaving them the first time. The shadows have gathered in the family room. Standing there in the grey, broken ghost of a home, watching you relive your past. Waiting for you to atone for your betrayal. Ma, Pa, the boys. Shadows now. Watching you break down, not realising the house around you is the musty and decrepit house you had walked into earlier, your eyes are playing tricks on you now.

They wait.

***

You hear your Pa call out behind you, but you lunge for the front door handle, pulling it open; you kick the screen door open and run into the dark night. You turn down the driveway, legs pumping as you speed past the barn—now a resplendent red—and inside you can hear the animals settling for the night. You follow the moonlight towards the main road. Just as you get close, you take a tumble. Your right foot, landing in a divot, sends you to the ground; you strike your head on a rock and everything fades out. When you open your eyes, you are in the house, lying on the floor in the daughter's—in your bedroom. Ma, Pa, and the boys are gone (well, you think) and everything is grey and covered in dust as before. Maybe you tripped over the small chest at the foot of the bed and knocked yourself out and dreamed the whole thing? No. You know that isn't true. You stand up slowly, your right ankle is throbbing. The house is dark now. You hobble out of the bedroom, towards the stairs, intent on making your way down to the front door; you don't want to spend the night here.

From outside, Bean starts barking. Which is impossible because *Bean isn't here anymore*. His pitch is high and tight. He is alerting you to something coming. You turn and head down towards the kitchen; unbolting the door, you step out onto the patio where Bean's kennel is. It is empty, but the barking is coming from the kennel. The shadows whimper and a force suddenly lifts you up and throws you back into the house, sending you flying across the kitchen. You crash into the oven, striking your head on the thick metal handle. In your mind, this is the final blow that breaks the chains around the box of memories. It opens and you know you are done for. You struggle to your feet, but the blows keep striking your chest, sending you down to the ground, so you try to crawl towards the hall. At the other end you can see them there now—the shadows. Four of them, huddled and watching as you now face what you had inflicted on them all those years ago.

The dolls were dropped on the bed and the flames extinguished, but not before burning the mattress. You were going to try something else to punish your parents for saying no. Dropping to your knees, you placed your hands on the carving and began to chant what you had read in the book. You chant hard and fast, eyes closed and willing it into being. You stop. Nothing. You can hear them talking about you downstairs. Your brothers are goofing off in the bathroom. Frustrated, you pull the rug over the carving and climb into bed. When they are all asleep, you will run away. No one will stop you from being with him. You are sixteen. You know what you want. Right?

Be careful what you wish for.

You are on your back now, clawing at the force that is gripping your throat. Tilting your head back, you see them there, still watching you. The grip releases and you gasp, the air burns as you suck it in, rolling over and trying to get up to run. A blow to your back, you drop. You get back up again. Another blow, you drop. You scramble to all fours only to be pinned by an excruciatingly crushing pressure to your torso; it pops your ribs one by one. You try to scream, but the only thing that comes from your mouth now is a trickle of blood.

In the dead of night, they slept. You got up and quietly fetched your backpack and tiptoed out onto the landing. The house was quiet save for the ticking of the grandfather clock that stood in the family room. You make your way downstairs, reaching the front door. On the porch you don't see the large dark shape that you had summoned earlier that night, there in the corner, waiting. You don't notice it watching you with dark red eyes. It moves by you quickly—quietly—slipping into the house as you pull the front door closed behind you. The night air was cool and crisp as you jog down the drive towards the main road. Your plan is to hitchhike into town to his place, and from there you will leave for a new life together, just as he had promised you. Halfway down the drive you hear Bean barking followed by the screams of your family, ending with a guttural growl followed by silence. You run now for the main road. You don't look back to see the flames that are engulfing the home.

You struggle to breathe, still trying to fight it. It grabs you by your legs and swings you into the walls.

Your family watches on.

You were picked up by the side of the road as dawn was breaking. By the time you reached town, you were elated to be free. You arrived on his doorstep and knocked, waiting with excitement to tell him that you could run away together now. The door opens, and it is a woman wearing one of his T-shirts. Your brain begins to pop as you work out what is going on. He appears behind her and asks you what you are doing there.

Your left arm is twisted and wrenched

from its socket.

You tell him that you are there to run away with him now. He laughs. She laughs. He tells the woman he doesn't know who you are, never seen you before in his life. He calls you little girl and they close the door in your face, leaving you humiliated. You want to go back home. Cop cars, followed by the fire trucks, come screaming by, sirens blaring and lights flashing. Heading in the direction of the farms. They found them. Your family. In pieces. It was a mess, apparently. The police found you wandering along the road out of town later that afternoon. You tell the police back at the station that you managed to flee the attacker. You couldn't save your brothers. You couldn't save your parents. You shake, you sob. The police officers' comfort you. You go to court. You tell the court what you told the police. The judge decides to send you to a hospital where you spend your days with doctors, learning how to move forward from the tragedy of losing your family. You get placed into a new family and you move on. You grow, you graduate, you get a career and a new life and every year you move forward, another chain is wrapped around the Pandora's Box in your mind.

But the dreams would come through. Of an abandoned farmhouse that looked so familiar to you. When you pulled over, you didn't see a house. You saw the hill it had been on. As you walked up the drive, from the ashes it appeared, restoring itself for you to come home. For everything you do, for everything you put out into the universe, it will always, always find its way back to you threefold. The blood is more than a trickle now—it is thick, and you are trying to spit it out, but the clots catch in your throat. Your left arm lies limp by your side, as you wait for the end. You can feel it breathing on the back of your head. You can see their feet; they stand in the doorway of the family room. The shadows of your family. A pressure bears down on your skull and you know now what they went through that night you ran down the drive, away from them. As you draw in your last breaths, you hear crackling and feel heat as flames begin to engulf the room around you.

***

By morning, there is an abandoned farm. The empty paddocks are full of weeds and grass as high as your waist. The driveway is littered with potholes and divots. You wouldn't drive your car along it, it would break the suspension. The grass and weeds ripple in the breeze, although if you were standing there, you would not be able to feel the breeze yourself. The area is silent, some say it is as if the land is trapped in a void for all eternity. The house had burned down over thirty years ago. Locals say the daughter, Maisie, had a hand in it, she was by all accounts a very spoiled young lady. She had fallen for a college kid in town and wanted to leave with him for a new life in California. He left town after she was arrested; no one has seen or heard from him since. Locals reported seeing a woman who looked a lot like an older Maisie in town the day before when she had stopped at the service station for fuel. No one spoke to her and she acted like she had never known that this town existed.

The police found her car this morning by the side of the road at the entrance to the abandoned farmstead. When they ventured onto the property, the place where the house and barn had once stood, they noticed the ground was smouldering and abnormally warm to the touch, but the ashes of the home and barn had long been gone.

They were unable to locate the woman.

RENDER UNTO CAESAR

By Liam Hogan

"Mr Odberry?"

A face appears in the thin gap between door and frame. Nose too big, lips too grey, eyes red and glistening.

"Mr Joseph Franklin Odberry?"

"Yes?" the rabbit at the doorway nervously replies.

I flash my ID card and give him a reassuring smile. "I'm Ms Adriana Prescott, from NHS Blood and Transplant. May I come in?"

"Is this...is this about my kidney?"

I nod, solemn now. "Yes. Yes, it is."

The inside of the council flat matches Mr Odberry. Like him, it is devoid of any hope, any colour, any future. It's dark, it smells, and it looks like it curled up to die sometime in the 1990s and somehow forgot to do the dying part. I perch primly on the edge of a frayed, brown sofa, while Mr Odberry peers from the depths of his easy chair.

"Now," I say, tapping on my tablet. "Just to confirm, Mr Odberry, you received a kidney transplant in June of last year, at Barts and the London. Is that correct?"

Mr Odberry jerks his head in assent.

"If you please, could you clearly say 'yes' or 'no'? For my records?"

"Y-yeah," he confirms, and I press the appropriate button on the electronic form.

"Thank you. Tell me, Mr Odberry, were you ever told who your donor was?"

He shakes his head and then, at my raised eyebrow, stutters a "N-no."

"Let me enlighten you. Your donor was a..." I carefully read the name, though I know it well enough. "Mr Sanjit Parul, declared deceased following a Road Traffic Accident on the 2nd June at 3:43 p.m."

Mr Odberry blinks owlishly up at me. No doubt, he fears whatever news I'm about to impart. I wonder what he imagines? Some case of malpractice? A recently uncovered medical issue with the donor? Or does he hope that this is just a routine checkup, albeit one without the customary month-in-advance appointment? I put him out of his misery.

"Well, Mr Odberry; Mr Parul would like his kidney back."

There's a small shake of the head. Disbelief. Perfectly understandable. "I thought..." The voice is almost lost in the dullness of the room and I have to strain to hear, "I thought you said he was...*deceased*?"

"Quite so. He was. But, after the

change to the laws as part of the Returnee Act, passed in April, he is nevertheless entitled to claim back any possessions he had at the time of his unfortunate death. And that does, I'm afraid, include his organs."

There's a look of realisation, of horror. "Mr Parul is a...a *zombie*?"

I wince. "Please, Mr Odberry! There's absolutely no call for the 'Z' word. Mr Parul is a *returnee*, legally registered as such."

"But...I need his kidney."

"I'm sure you do. However, Mr Parul has a priori right. And, before you point out that removing his kidney may well kill you, I'd like you to note that even though Mr Parul was dead when the organ was taken from him, removing it was surely done in such a way as would have led to his certain demise, were he alive at the time. So it does all rather balance out."

There's a pause while Mr Odberry does his best to process this. He blinks. He shifts as if his chair, the one moulded to his desiccated form, has suddenly become ill fitting. Uneasy. At an educated guess, he withdrew into his council-flat shell shortly after his operation and hoped everything and everyone would stay away, thus missing the bulk of the news about the End of the World.

Finally he manages, in a strangled voice, to utter, "You're here to remove my kidney?"

"Heavens no, Mr Odberry!" I laugh.

"Do I look like a surgeon? I'm here merely to inform you of proceedings and to answer any questions you may have. The date for the operation is set for Tuesday-week. I do hope that is convenient?"

He gulps. Surprised, I suppose, at the speed. But, if it were done...

"I, um...will there be a replacement?"

"Ah," I frown and do my best to show sympathy. "Well, obviously, the NHS is rather stretched at the moment, with much of our current effort dedicated to returning organs to returnee donors. So there's a halt on all transplants, I'm afraid. You see, unless we know for certain that the donor won't be returning—if, for example, his remains are to be cremated—we rather have to assume that he might still want his—or her!—organs back."

Mr Odberry has turned a most peculiar shade. It's almost reassuring to see that his doughy skin can still adopt a colour, any colour, though green wouldn't have been my first choice. He gasps for air.

I hurry to reassure him. "What the NHS can do—subject to your approval—is inoculate you with the Lazarus virus."

"I'd...I'd become a zombie?"

I wince again. Really, the gutter press has a lot to answer for. I thought we'd moved on from such brain-dead prejudice, particularly as the previously deceased now outnumber those who were alive at the start of the outbreak. Which was why the Act had been so swiftly passed; to buy their precious votes.

"A return*ee*, Mr Odberry! Though, strictly, if you're inoculated before the operation, you'd never *actually* die, so there would be no issue with your retaining your status as a living, never deceased, being."

He doesn't look particularly cheered by the thought. I guess it's hard adjusting to this brave new world.

I sigh. "It is, of course, entirely your own decision."

He nods distractedly, his breath coming in short wheezes. The green has taken on a yellowish tinge. I half wonder if I should be calling for an ambulance.

"And I'll be okay, will I? If I'm infec…inoculated?"

He's grasping at straws, bless.

"You'll remain alive... But as for healthy, well, *no*. Not without a working kidney, necrotic or otherwise. The timing has rather conspired against you, Mr Odberry. If you were diagnosed with organ failure today, they'd simply inoculate you and send you on your way. The virus would reanimate your diseased flesh and the body's natural repair system would do the rest. Assuming you stayed off the drink, of course!"

He blushes at that, which means he's now pretty much covered the full spectrum; just blue missing. That might yet come. I suspect Mr Odberry has ignored his physician's advice to 'never touch another drop.' And, if so, Mr Parul might have a legal case for damages, if neglect could be proven. But as Mr Parul was—and presumably still is—tea-total, it shouldn't do him any *lasting* damage.

"So what happens to me?"

"Well, you never know," I say, brightly. "They're scouring the medical labs and pathology museums. Perhaps they'll fit you out with something from Victorian times? I hear the Lazarus virus can bring even such antique specimens back to a semblance of life. And of course, there are benefits."

"Benefits?"

"Oh, indeed. Since the Human Tissue Act doesn't apply to specimens over a hundred years old, you can opt to have a Perspex window put in, if you like. With medical schools suffering a severe shortage of cadavers—ones who sit still, anyway!—you can earn a small but regular fee simply for letting trainee doctors look in on your kidney. And then there are body-parties..."

I let my patter trail off. I don't think Mr Odberry is the sort to exhibit himself in that way. Business like, I conclude, "So, if I can just get your signature that we've had this little talk and you've taken note of your appointment date, I'll be on my way."

He fumbles with the stylus, his signature running wild across the slippery glass screen. Doesn't matter. It still counts. Gladly, I get up, ready to go.

"Actually, Mr Parul would like to thank you," I say as I brush the back of my skirt, checking that no residue of Mr Odberry's flat remains.

"Thank me?" he echoes.

"Oh yes. While his kidney has kept you alive, you, in return, have kept his kidney healthy. Or healthier than it would have been, if it were rotting in a grave for six months! We're finding that of all the formerly deceased, organ donors are the ones who end up with the best quality of life. Once they get their organs back, of course!"

As the door snibs shut behind me, I step into the bright sunshine, breathing deep. The list of Mr Parul's still-to-be-reclaimed organs dictates the rest of my working day. A Northern colleague has already ticked off his liver, which found its way up to Manchester, but the rest of his body parts are scattered around London.

Next up is his other kidney, in Lewisham. Then double corneas over in Hampstead. And, to finish the day, his pancreas, somewhere near Bethnal Green.

But I can afford a brief respite before I set off. A moment to absorb the sun's warming rays, chasing away the grey of Mr Odberry's dreary flat. All in all, *far* too reminiscent of my re-awakening, two months back: cold, and dark, and six feet below.

First published by Fundead Publications, 2017

COROCOTTA ROAD

By Patrick J. Gallagher

"You're kidding, right?"

"Nope, the ritual requires blood." Ben grinned as he said it, enjoying the look of discomfort on Nicola's face. She folded her arms defensively, keeping her hands tucked away.

"It's an urban myth, not a ritual," said Jake. "Nothing's going to happen no matter what we do."

"Are you sure of that?" replied Ben. "I mean, how can we really know if we don't follow the requirements exactly?"

"I swear to God, sometimes I wonder why I hang around with you idiots." Katy was sitting against the bonnet of the car. Ben had to squint to see her, positioned in between the headlights of his aging and battered Ford Laser.

"A lack of viable alternatives in a town this size, probably," observed Jake.

Katy snorted and stepped forward. "Tell me about it." She looked at Ben. "Okay genius, what do we have to do?"

"And why the blood?" asked Nicola.

"According to the legend, the car has to be marked with the blood of all the occupants; otherwise, it won't work," explained Ben. He produced a small pocketknife. "Who wants to go first?"

"Jesus, you're serious, aren't you?" said Katy. "Where the hell did you come up with this shit?"

Ben unfolded the blade of the knife, milking the moment by examining the gleam of the metal. "I saw it in an old newspaper article from the sixties. The Beast of Corocotta Road. It was a big thing for a while at the time. Then it looks like everybody just forgot about it."

He pressed the point of the blade against his thumb, producing a large bead of blood, then rubbed his thumb and forefinger together, smearing the blood around. Stepping up to the car, he pressed his thumb against the bonnet, leaving a bloody print on the dull white paintwork. He turned to the others.

"Who's next?" he asked, holding up the knife.

Nicola took a step back. Jake shrugged and held out his hand. "Let's do it."

Ben pricked Jake's thumb with the knife, smirking as Jake twitched and muttered, "Ow." Once the second bloody thumbprint was added to the car, Katy took the knife from Ben's hand.

"Hey," he objected.

Katy wiped the blade against the sleeve of Ben's shirt. "If you think I'm letting you near me with a knife, you're crazy." She drew blood without flinching, added her print to the car, then held the knife out to Nicola.

"Does it hurt?" Nicola asked.

"A small prick," replied Katy with a grin. "Kinda like Ben."

"Ooh, burn," snickered Jake.

Ben scowled. "Can we just get on with it?"

Nicola reluctantly held her hand out to Katy, who applied the point of the knife to her thumb in one quick jab, drawing a minimal amount of blood. Nicola pressed her thumb onto the bonnet, then immediately pulled out a tissue and wrapped it around the thumb.

"Alright, let's do this!" said Ben,

eagerly rubbing his hands together.

Katy rolled her eyes. "Jesus."

They piled into the car, Ben and Jake in the front, Katy and Nicola in the back. Ahead of them, the headlights illuminated a few dozen metres of the road, curving off into pitch blackness, scraggly eucalyptus trees crowding in on either side.

In the rear-view mirror, Ben could see the T-intersection branching off the main road, lit by a single ancient streetlight.

"Okay. It's about ten K's from here to the highway. According to the legend, if the Beast comes after us, we have to make it past the stop sign at that intersection to be safe."

"Yeah, whatever. Just get on with it," sighed Katy from behind him.

"Everybody buckle up. There might not be a Beast, but there might be cops."

Ben threw the car into gear, and they started off along the narrow bitumen road. The streetlight of the intersection was soon hidden from view as they rounded the first bend. Now the only light was the bright cone extending ahead of them from the headlights. To either side, the passing trees were faint, flickering shadows.

"Keep your eyes open," Ben told the others. Beside him, Jake had pulled out his phone, getting it ready to record. He checked their speed. A steady eighty.

"I hope we don't hit any 'roos," Nicola murmured from the back seat. Ben looked at her in the rear-view mirror. She still had her arms wrapped around herself, pointedly trying not to look out the window beside her, reluctant to face the dark night flowing past them. Ben grinned as he shifted his gaze forward again. She was…

His eyes flicked back to the mirror, and he frowned. "Hey, does anybody else see that behind us?"

"Oh, hah-bloody-hah," said Katy.

"No, I'm serious. Look."

The others twisted in their seats to peer out the rear window. For a few moments, the only sound was the thrum of the car's engine.

"What is that?" breathed Jake.

Somewhere along the road behind them, beyond the faint glow of the car's tail lights, two bright red pinpoints of light bobbed along, keeping pace with the car.

No, not keeping pace, thought Ben, risking another glance in the mirror…

They were gaining, getting closer.

There was a tremor in Nicola's voice. "They look like eyes…"

Even Katy didn't sound so sure of herself. "I swear to God, Ben, this better not be some stupid joke of yours."

Jake was trying to brace his arm against the headrest so that he could capture the lights on camera. "I think I'd prefer if it was a joke," he said.

As the car rounded another bend, the lights were lost to them. Ben pressed his foot down a bit further on the accelerator, pushing their speed up to a hundred. He was no longer grinning. The fun was starting to fade from their little adventure.

Jake checked his phone. "Crap, I couldn't hold it steady enough to catch anything."

"What do you think it was?" asked Katy.

Jake shrugged. "At a guess, probably the reflection of our taillights off a road sign."

"I don't remember passing any signs," observed Ben.

"Ow, hey, Nic. Ease up." In the back seat, Nicola had clutched Katy's hand. Her grip was growing tighter, her nails digging into Katy's skin, as she stared out the passenger side window. She was exhaling in short, sharp gasps.

"Nic?"

Katy followed Nicola's gaze out the

window into the almost complete darkness. Her eyes widened. "Oh shit. Guys…"

Jake looked out the window. "No way…"

Ben leaned forward to see past Jake. Flickering as they passed behind the trees lining the road were the two red lights that had just been following behind them. Now they were running parallel to the car, bobbing up and down slightly with a steady fluid motion.

Instinctively, he pushed down even further on the accelerator, the aging engine protesting as their speed crept past a hundred and twenty kilometres an hour.

The lights continued to keep pace with the car.

"They really are eyes," murmured

Nicola.

"They can't be," said Jake. "It's gotta be a drone or something." He rolled down the window, the warm night air immediately blasting into the car.

"What are you doing?" asked Katy.

"Listen."

Beyond the sound of the car as it raced through the night, they all heard it. A rhythmic thumping, punctuated by the crunch and splintering of wood, as something large pounded through the scrub alongside them.

"That does *not* sound like a drone," said Katy. "Ben, go faster. Get us out of here."

Ben shook his head. "We're doing a hundred and thirty, and I'm flat to the floor.

This is all we've got."

Ahead, the trees along the road thinned slightly for a short stretch. As they reached the clearer area, the thing keeping pace with them took the opportunity to move in closer. Ben saw the lights, that he still held a vague hope weren't really eyes, grow larger.

And then it was on the road alongside them.

The faint backwash of the headlights was enough to illuminate the horror. It was a hound with matted grey-black fur; the eyes, blazing red-hot coals. And it was massive, easily as tall as the car.

Steam rose from its back as it loped along, easily keeping pace with them. The head was half turned towards them, watching both the car and the road ahead. Its paws thumped against the bitumen.

Nicola let out an involuntary scream. Jake pushed himself back from the open window, pressing against Ben, making it hard to steer.

"Faster!" shouted Katy. "Go faster!"

As Ben tried to coax more speed from the straining engine, the Beast moved in closer. It suddenly swerved sharply towards the car, crashing into the side with the bulk of its body. Nicola's window exploded in a shower of fragmented safety glass, eliciting another scream.

The force of the impact pushed the car sideways. Ben struggled with the steering, just managing to keep them on the road.

The Beast dropped back behind the

car, and for a moment Ben thought that they might have a chance of escaping. Then it shifted course slightly and came pounding forward again, this time on the driver's side.

The massive head drew level with Ben's window, and sheer panic coursed through his body. It was so close. It turned to look directly at him with its bright glowing eyes, the window steaming up from its huffing breath.

It rammed the car again. Ben heard himself swear as he tried to compensate for the sudden shift. The front tyre on his side of the car shredded itself from the sideways force. The rubber separated from the rim with a sharp jolt and sparks flew into the night air as the metal screamed along the road.

Worst of all, the car slowed.

Ben's knuckles turned white on the wheel. He began to rock back and forth, tears streaming down his face, urging the battered vehicle to give him more speed. The cries and screams of the others were a meaningless cacophony around him.

Having done its damage, the Beast dropped back again, then once again rushed forward, returning to Jake's side of the car.

Jake tried to push himself as far from his side of the car as possible. "Here it comes again!"

The warning cut through the panic and gave Ben a moment to brace for the impact. As the car shuddered from the hit, he managed to maintain better control of the car. But the trade-off was a greater degree of damage as the structure absorbed the full force of the blow.

Metal buckled along the side of the car, destroying the integrity of the passenger door. It flew open, hanging by a twisted hinge.

Ben could feel the car fighting him every inch of the way, now. The damage it had sustained made it almost impossible to control. One more hit and they were done for.

His brain feverishly tried to calculate how far they still had to travel. The highway couldn't be too far away. If the legend held true, they only had to make it past the stop sign at the intersection, and they'd be safe from the Beast.

The steering wheel was shuddering in his hands as they still sped along at over a hundred kilometres an hour. Even so, he knew they weren't going to make it. If he didn't want to die tonight, he knew he had to find some way to slow the Beast down, maybe distract it, just for a few seconds…

Jake was reaching out, trying to grab the mangled door and drag it shut. He was straining against the constraint of the seatbelt, leaning out into the night.

Before he could let himself think about what he was doing, Ben reached down and unclipped Jake's seatbelt, then shoved him towards the open door. Jake didn't even have time to cry out as he tumbled out of the car. Ben saw his body bounce and roll along the road in the rear-view mirror.

The Beast immediately slowed, turning its attention to the sprawled figure on the road. As the car rounded a bend, he caught a last look at the massive creature locking its jaws around Jake's head.

Behind him, Katy and Nicola were frozen in shock.

"What…what did you just do?" gasped Katy.

"I didn't have a choice," snapped Ben. "If I didn't do something, we were all going to die!"

As the road straightened out of the curve, he saw the light of the highway intersection up ahead. They were going to make it.

"Turn around!" screamed Katy. "We have to go back for Jake!"

"We're almost there!" replied Ben. The intersection was drawing ever closer. Safety and survival beckoned.

Katy released the clasp of her seatbelt and lunged forward, grasping for the steering wheel. "Turn around, you bastard!"

The car swerved sharply to the left as they fought for control of the steering wheel. They were heading off the road. Ben yanked the steering wheel back to the right.

Too hard…

The overcompensation caused the car to slew sideways. There was a moment of weightlessness as it became airborne, then the world exploded around Ben as glass shattered and metal warped as the car hit the ground on its side.

He was vaguely aware of Katy tumbling past him, towards the open passenger door. Then the car continued its roll, and she was gone.

The tumbling continued, smashing Ben and Nicola against the crumpling frame despite their seatbelts, before finally coming to rest on its roof. Then there was near silence, the only sounds the ticking of hot metal rapidly cooling and Ben's desperate, gasping breaths.

He was alive. Hanging upside down from his seatbelt, but alive. He braced himself against the roof with one hand, then used the other to undo the seatbelt. As he hit the ground, an intense bolt of pain shot through his right leg.

He twisted around in the confines of

the wreckage. "Nicola…?"

Nicola still hung from her seatbelt, eyes wide and staring. Most of the skin had been torn from one side of her face from the impact against the road through her open window. Her neck looked twisted and extended.

Ben fought back the urge to vomit. He frantically dragged himself out through the now missing door, onto the warm tarmac of the road. Fragments of glass cut into his hands.

Back down the road, he could see Katy's body sprawled in an expanding pool of blood. There was only a mess of gore and hair where her head should have been.

Sobbing, he tried to take stock of his own condition and was horrified to see the large shard of bloody bone sticking through the leg of his pants. There was strangely little pain.

He looked up and saw the stop sign marking the intersection looming above him. Despite everything, a wave of elation swept through him. He'd made it. He was still alive and had reached the intersection. He was safe from the Beast.

Then he looked down and saw the solid white line of the intersection painted across the road.

Still at least a metre in front of him.

He heard heavy panting approaching behind him, felt hot, foul breath on the back of his neck. Even as he turned his head, every fibre of his being was screaming at him not to do it, to just crawl as fast as he could towards the white line.

Huge yellow fangs, with a pit of darkness beyond, rushed towards his face.

LA FLOR

By Patrick Winters

The night was brimming with dark potential; the *bruja* knew this, and she walked into the desert to seek it out.

A half-moon cast its glow upon the valley, the Sonoran sands that were a golden-brown in the day now a mystic swath of grey and blue in the approaching twilight. The scattering of countless stars in the cobalt-coloured sky only added to the spectacular illumination of the sprawling vista. The winds had stilled the moment the sun sunk below the horizon; still, there was a stirring in the air—an ethereal shifting that tickled at the skin and sent a chill across the spine.

Withered bushes and spiny cacti sprouted up from the earth here and there, their silhouettes stretching across the landscape like tombstones across a barren graveyard. All manner of creatures which called this place home lay out of sight, curled away in their bushes and underground holes. Even the predators of the land—the snakes, the coyotes, the lizards—were tucked away in their secretive abodes, neither their hunger nor their mischievous ways incentive enough to creep through the darkness of this night.

To an outsider, it seemed a serene picture of night-time beauty and wonder, the like of which was only ever seen on postcards and travel shows; but to Ximena, a practitioner of black magic—one who knew of the world beside our own, the realm of long-forgotten gods and wandering spirits—it was a dwelling place of dark and otherworldly forces. And those forces were precisely what she wished to commune with.

Something within her stained soul could sense the ebb and flow of the earth's energies—pulses that carried her on her trek, like a ship adrift upon an ocean. And with that phantom tide came whispers from the other side. Whispers that coaxed her onwards, tempting her with hushed promises of reprisal. And if she could appease them with her offering and her spells, they might stretch their voices down to darker depths, where they could utter her pleas into powerful ears.

A couple—husband and wife tourists from Nebraska, according to their license plate—had supplied her with the fresh bones she'd needed. They'd stopped off at the rundown gas station she attended the night before, their cameras snapping quick shots of the joint and the scenic views of nature about them. You'd think they'd never seen sand before, the way they grinned out at the horizon, that look of goofy adventure and discovery that only tourists could conjure smacked across their cheery faces.

Ximena could still hear the woman's screams as she gutted the husband. She'd used her cherished knife to do it, the one that had been passed down from mother to daughter in her *familia* since before the white man set foot on the shores of her people's homeland. The blade had been made from wicked-sharp obsidian, chipped from the solidified flow of a long-gone volcano that, upon its eruption, had swallowed up a village of nearly two hundred souls. The accursed stone had pierced the husband's stomach easily enough. Then she'd turned the knife on the wife, the blade finding its mark even quicker with her much softer flesh. Technically, the bones she needed for this ritual only had to come from a single person—the man, preferably; such spells always worked better with men, it seemed. But it would've been a shame to separate the couple, and the knife—along with Ximena's furious soul—had yearned for bloodshed.

So much red—scarlet and warm, like the sheets we slept in that first night together...

After carving into the man's chest with her blade, Ximena had snapped off a few pairs of his ribs for use in the ritual. She'd dragged the bodies into the desert and left them there, where they would be eaten by animals or buried in the whipping winds and piling sands of the next day. The desert had its ways of concealing secrets, after all, and Ximena was certain the couple would be no more missed than a grain of dirt fallen from atop an anthill. And after she'd dropped their car off at her cousin's chop-shop, she'd gone home and slept soundly, sensing her revenge was at hand.

He called me su flor—*his flower…*

Ximena shoved the bittersweet thought aside and pushed on, letting the forces of the night guide her to whatever spot they saw fit—wherever the barrier between worlds was thinnest, and where she could see to her ritual. After a few more minutes of wandering, she found the place she was seeking; it was in a cleared patch of dirt, encircled by black, scraggly bushes. She came to a stop the moment she set foot in the ring, unable to move any further, as though the hand of Fate itself held her to the spot.

Ximena dropped her backpack and set about her preparations. She could feel the spirits of that neighbouring realm gathering around her, watching her work.

She arranged and tied up some sturdy branches in the centre of this unholy spot, from which she hung the pot she had hoisted along. Then she collected some brush, piling it up and lighting it. The ingredients for the ritual came next; she pulled them out of her backpack one by one, adding them to the pot. Water. Herbs.

Vulture's urine. The venom of a Chihuahuan night snake. She let it all simmer while she saw to the bones of the tourist, scattering them in a stone bowl and using her hammer on them, pounding the ribs into dust and red-stained chips. And with each strike, another memory came back to her:

Mateo, saying he loved her for the first time.

A heated argument, which led to their first breakup.

The both of them naked and sighing in his bed, lost in ecstasy and reconciliation.

Another argument—curses flying and the back of his hand finding her cheek.

A bundle of flowers, an apology, and another sweaty night to follow.

Finding a love-note in his truck from some *puta* she'd never heard of.

The adamant denial, Mateo saying it was just some stupid joke, and that she was the only lover in his life.

The phone calls taken in secret, his whispers reaching her ears even from the other room. All the texts, coming in and going out as he sat beside her on the couch, watching television. Finding the boxes of condoms hidden away at his place—colours and flavours she hadn't been seeing or tasting for herself.

All of the passions and inequities of her tryst with Mateo were fighting it out—yet again, even now. But she knew which of them would win out, and her blows to the bones grew heavier with the building of her rage. The cycle of forgiveness and doubt would end with tonight's deed, and irrevocably so, if only the gods would hear her and bestow their aid…

The bones were ready now; but more importantly, *she* was ready.

Ximena stood and strode over to the fire, dumping the crushed up remains into the bubbling pot. A strange smoke arose as the mixture was completed, and that tingling sensation that'd been teasing her body pierced down into her very core, filling her with a dark vigour.

Ximena stepped back and knelt before the fire, her heart pounding like a war drum. She began to sway to and fro, mumbling incantations first spoken in ages past. Then, once the words were said, she bowed down and set her palms across the dirt, like the devout at prayer, and spoke aloud her desires to the one she wished to invoke: Mictlāntēcutli—lord of the Underworld and the great god of Death.

"Spirits of the dark, carry my cry to the depths beneath this world! I beg benefaction from the King of Mictlan, render of souls and master of the dead! Let my call ring through the nine levels of your kingdom! See my offering, and witness my devotion to you!"

Her invocation grew fiercer, and her skin burned with the fire of her fury.

"I seek your power, Lord! I seek death! The one I loved has struck me. Cursed me. Betrayed me. And I'll abide it *no longer*!"

Tears overflowed in her shut eyes, but

there was no sorrow in them. Only wrath.

"I wish him to suffer. To be *unmade*. To feel an end that only your might can bring! And in return, I offer you his soul to feed upon—and my own, to serve you in this life and the next, in whatever way you wish. I beg you, dark one—grant me my request!"

She rose up, scrawling sigils in the dirt at her knees and reciting other words of magic, completing the black rite. And when it was done, she screamed into the night:

"Hear me and answer!"

Her cry echoed through the dark. As it rang in her ears, her heart's wild beat eased, and the energies swirling about her faded to whence they'd come.

She waited—but only a moment longer. For soon enough, the dirt before her began to rise up, swelling into a small mound which split and cracked open. And from out of the earth, a grey stem rose up, slinking about like a snake and sprouting little nubs which gradually shaped and curved into wicked-looking thorns.

From the stem's tip, blackened petals burst forth, blooming into a flower the likes of which this world had never seen— horribly withered but strangely beautiful; dead, yet promising new life. A new life for Ximena—one where her broken heart was mended by recompense, and the one who'd broken it received his just reward.

Smiling, Ximena traced her fingertips along the flower's petals. They were smooth to the touch, and the tantalising sensation cooled her heated flesh, sending goose bumps all over her body.

As she cradled the flower in her palms, the whispers from the other side struck up again. They told Ximena what needed to be done, and with each word, her smile grew.

***

The plan was simple and getting Mateo to her place was even simpler. All she had to do was call him up and say she wanted him to come over. It didn't matter that she'd said she never wanted to see him again just three days before. After all, she'd said that to him plenty of times, and whether she'd taken it back or he'd won her over again with some tequila and charm, it never stuck.

He was knocking on her front door come six o'clock that evening, right on cue. When she answered the door, he was standing straight and tall on the other side, not a care in the world showing on that handsome and stubble-covered face of his. And he must have been in the mood to "make up" with her, because he had a brand new bottle of Espolòn in hand.

The skeletal figure on the label inspired a knowing smirk from Ximena, which Mateo must have mistaken for a show of affection.

"So," he said with that devilish grin of his, "I guess this means we're back in the saddle together."

Ximena, wanting to scratch his eyes out right then and there, took the bottle from him instead. She opened her door wider and aimed for as gentle a tone as she could manage. "Our ride isn't over yet. Come on in."

He leaned in and kissed her on the temple, and she clenched her jaw, wondering who else had been feeling his lips as of late. "*Maravilloso, mi flor,*" he whispered in her ear. Then he slipped past her, heading for the kitchen.

She went into the living room and plopped down on her couch. Mateo came in a moment later, carrying two glasses and settling down beside her. He opened up the tequila and poured for the both of them—making sure her glass was filled to the top—and he charged right into the motions.

The flirtations and the promises. The compliments and the declarations. Mixing dashes of humiliation with stretches of bravado. Xemina listened to it all and more, letting him do most of the talking, only interjecting to coax some more out of him—secretly prodding, playing with him the way a cat would paw at a dead bird it would eventually gobble up. And as she listened, she realised she'd heard every word of this before. Repeatedly, actually, and across numerous nights. But unlike before, she realised just how hollow it all was. That it was blatant bullshit, measured out and spoon-fed to keep their tryst strung along, ensuring he'd have her warm thighs to fall into whenever he wanted, or whenever his other little *panochas* wouldn't give him what he wanted. The realisation set her blood to boiling and her gut to roiling, but she kept up her fake smiles and obliging little laughs—until she couldn't take it any longer.

After Mateo had turned the conversation back to himself, complaining about some *gringo* he'd dealt with at work that day, Ximena saw her opening. She set her glass aside, having only taken sips from it in all that time, and stood up. "It sounds like you need a pick-me-up," she said. "And I have just the thing you need."

She went over to the mantle of her fireplace and grabbed a plain white gift box that was sitting there. As she brought it back over to the couch, Mateo gave her a look, his brow turned up in a bit of surprise, but cracking a grin. He seemed a tad cautious, but she'd clearly piqued his curiosity. "What's this?"

"Just something I'd like you to have." She handed him the box and sat down—in her recliner, a safe distance across from him.

Mateo tilted his head in a show of mock uncertainty, but when she gave him a nod to go ahead, he smiled and set to opening the gift.

He gave a questioning look to what lay inside: her special black flower, surrounded by white tissue paper, and nothing more.

"Uhm, thanks?" Mateo mumbled. He looked like a defeated child who'd just received socks for Christmas. "What inspired this?"

Ximena's eyes went wide as he reached down into the box. His fingers went right to the stem, pushing aside the tissue paper. And just as she'd hoped, he couldn't see the flower's thorns. A second later he cried out, pulling his hand back and putting a pricked finger up to his mouth.

Ximena grinned, seeing a droplet of red spreading along the white tissue paper in the box. Mateo saw that show of joy, and his anger instantly flared. The Latin lover façade shattered like so much glass.

"The hell are you smiling about? You think me getting cut is funny?"

Ximena sighed in victory and shook her head. "Oh no, *cerdo*, but what comes next—that'll be *muy gracioso*."

A fire rose up in Mateo's eyes, and he jumped up from the couch. He took a couple steps forward, raising his hand to deliver one of his slaps—but he stopped when he noticed the state of that hand. An inky darkness was spreading beneath his skin, spiralling through veins and painting his muscles with haste, the whole of his pricked finger already gone pitch black and the rest of his hand following suit. He clenched his hand, a flash of pain marring his mask of disbelief, and the blackness just kept climbing his arm.

"What the hell is this?" he groaned, his teeth gritting and a tear forming at the corner of his eye. He looked over to her in rising fear. "What the hell have you done to me?"

Ximena leaned back in the recliner and crossed her legs. "The worst thing I could manage. I just hope it'll hurt as bad as I want it to."

Mateo cringed as another flare of pain swept over him, and now the blackness was creeping up his neck and over his chest. His mouth gaped open in a silent scream, and he stumbled forward, collapsing to his knees. He started to convulse and writhe, curling up in the fetal position one moment, then going straight and stiff as a board the next. It took another minute for the entirety of his skin to go a glossy black, and another five for what happened next.

Mateo was decaying before Ximena's very eyes. Slowly, painfully. His flesh cracked open and flaked off, eroding like a mountain beneath the pressure of time. And as his skin began to crumble away, she was afforded a look at his innards, the bones of his failing body growing brittle and snapping while his organs corroded with an acidic bubbling.

His handsome face gawked up at her as the process worked its agonizing magic, his cheeks shrivelling up and his eyes turning sunken, becoming a ghostly caricature of the man he used to be.

Eventually, he was just a pathetic husk mewling at her feet; then, once Mictlāntēcutli's bane wound down to its end, there was nothing left of Mateo but a pile of his clothes and the grey dust of his body.

Ximena lounged there a while more, savouring the moment and trying to put a name to what she was feeling. "Release" seemed apt, and she relished in the word. Then she went into the kitchen and grabbed a broom and dustpan. She swept Mateo's remains into the pan, and she added the dust of the fateful black flower to the mix. It had withered like its victim, right there on her couch, without her even noticing. That was a shame; she'd hoped to keep it as a memento—something to remind her of who Mateo *really* was, if she were ever stupid enough to try to remember him better.

Once that was done, Ximena went into

her backyard. A hard eastern wind struck up the moment she stepped outside, and she threw Mateo into the air, letting it carry him off in a whipping cloud of grey.

She'd throw away his clothes and take his truck to her cousin's chop-shop later on. And then she'd wait to see what the great and terrible Mictlāntēcutli would ask of her for his aid.

But for now, she'd enjoy the approaching dusk—and the freedom that came with it.

THE SWAMP'S EYES

By Thomas Sturgeon Jr.

Out in this feverish swamp, sweat dripping down his brow, David swatted a mosquito aside. He enjoyed hunting for alligator's in the Louisiana river as much as any other hunter, but he and Sonny weren't having any luck at all. The boat was slow-moving due to a hole in the middle that they had overlooked that morning.

"Damn, we're leaking, man! We need to find land as quickly as possible. Otherwise, we'll have to carry the fucking boat in these gator-infested waters. And there're poisonous snakes, too," Sonny said as he smoked a Marlboro Red cigarette, trying to stay calm.

From out of nowhere, a monstrous scream could be heard in the distance. Sonny and David stood up, full of fear and tension.

"What the hell was that?!" Sonny asked.

"Don't know, and don't want to find out. Land's not too far away. Maybe we can make a swim for it?"

"Nope, man. These waters are too damned dangerous. Push as hard as you can," Sonny said as they peddled the oars of the boat towards land.

They had the feeling that they were being watched, but by what?

There were a couple of snakes hanging from the trees as both men peddled to shore. Two alligators followed them to land as they jumped from the boat onto the marshy grass and ran as fast as they could, making their way back to their truck.

They got lost along the way—night had fallen on the swamp as they trudged through the mud by the trees.

A blood-curdling scream could be heard throughout the swamplands. They shone their flashlights on a reptile-like cryptid of some sort. The creature stared them down, eyes glowing and evil red.

Hypnotised by its gaze, the men fell to the ground and the creature ate them both, tearing off chunks of flesh. The creature had been watching them since they arrived on the boat that morning. Dinner was served.

The reptile shifted into the shape of a woman. She screamed, and the alligators crawled to the hunters' corpses and ate what had remained.

The woman remained in the shadows of the swamp, waiting for hunters who would hurt her precious brothers and sisters. She was the swamp's eyes.

Be careful in the swamps or you too

will be the next meal for the Gator Witch.

ANIMAL KILLERS IN CHERRY FALLS

By Jacqueline Moran Meyer

Cherry Falls Community Facebook Page

Monday

Chase_Fairchild: Will we ever learn?

Our community has now entered a new barbaric low. I am sickened beyond all reason to report that the USDA Wildlife Services has confirmed the murder of a coyote in the Rocky Hills section of town.

Other communities can claim ignorance, but not ours. We knew there were other options that were not lethal.

James_Gray: Chase, I am a trapper. I know you are not. Coyotes can't be relocated.

Alexis_Cowel: Several dogs have been taken from their backyards in the Rocky Hills area. One dog was attacked with the owner nearby. When the homeowner screamed bloody murder, the animal dropped the dog and left. I believe the wildlife services were contacted to determine if this was typical behaviour.

Chase_Fairchild: Alexis, this was a cruel killing of an innocent animal. Animals act on instinct. What was done in Rocky Hills was a cold, calculated murder.

Michelle_Smythe: Having small children, I'm scared. The coyote may have rabies or no fear of humans.

Robert_Mondle: Who was the owner? How far away was the owner?

Simone_Clay: If the dog wasn't leashed, it's the owner's fault.

Janet_Simone: I don't appreciate the leash shaming. Does anyone care that my precious dog was attacked? I am not even sure what I saw; it happened so fast. I don't think it was a coyote, so I don't know how Chase heard one was killed. I am putting a night vision camera outside. Yes, Chase, animals act on instinct. My instinct told me that this creature, whatever it is, was aggressive. I don't want anyone to get hurt. Be careful.

Chase_Fairchild: Except the innocent coyotes.

Janet_Simone: Listen, Chase. I am a vegan, for God's sake. My homeowner's association, not me, approached the Wildlife Services. The professionals determine whether trapping is necessary or not. They are ASKED, not TOLD what to do. I believe they have more credentials than you, in making these decisions.

Chase_Fairchild: Coyote killer.

Janet_Simone: Wow…Karen… I mean Chase. You're evil and nuts. Do you wear leather, put down mice traps or eat meat? Wait until this hairy and hulking fanged thing turns up in your yard. Talk to me then.

3-responses

Tuesday

Chief_Marshall: Several dog attacks and missing dogs were reported yesterday. It's unclear what type of animals are doing this, as the descriptions vary, but there are many of them. The people involved fear public bullying if they come forward. I don't mean to be an alarmist, but we don't know what we are dealing with. Please report any sightings. Keep your children and pets inside. If you do need to be outside, walk with pepper spray, a bat, and/or a whistle.

Chase_Fairchild: I mean no disrespect, but this fear mongering is beneath you, Chief Marshall. Coyotes do not attack people. I am sending my kids out to play.

120-responses

Wednesday

Janet_Simone: I sent my night vision wildlife tape to the Wildlife Services and to Chief Marshall. The film was grainy and, frankly, it's impossible to believe what I saw was real. I have never creatures like them. Stay safe.

Peter_Fife: Janet, now who's nuts. You are just covering yourself.

Chase_Fairchild: I wouldn't trust your video.

Janet_Simone: Please. I am trying to help. And yes, not that you asked, my dog is O.K.

800-responses

Thursday

Chief_Marshall: School is cancelled. Two children were playing in their backyard. When the parent went in to get a cell phone, strange growls and screams were heard. She ran out and, unfortunately, her children were gone. Please keep a lookout for Chase Fairchild's children,

Petunia and Apollo.

Sara_Lehman: Terrible.

Janet_Simone: Were the kids leashed?

Terri_Richards: Janet, you are sick. Not funny.

Janet_Simone: No one cared about my dog, who is part of my family. If we listened to each other maybe this all could have been prevented.

1040-responses

Friday

Terri_Richards: Wtf were those horrifying noises last night? Did anyone else hear it?

Sara_Lehman: Yes. Terrifying

6097-responses

Chief_Marshall: Terrible news. The remains of Chase Fairchild's children have been identified. The animal bites cannot be recognized as any animal in the area. Please continue to report sightings. We are instituting a town lockdown until we know what we are dealing with. Everyone must stay indoors until further notice.

Janet_Simone: Omg.

20087-Responses

Saturday

No Activity

Sunday

No Activity

Sunday

Chief_Marshall: If you are reading this, stay away from windows, turn off all lights and/or barricade yourselves in a windowless room.

There is a national state of emergency. It's unclear what the creatures are but I truly believe they are not of this world.

God help us.

0-responses

SATAN'S APOCALYPSE

By Kevin J. Kennedy

When everything ended, I was just a kid. I wouldn't say I was too young to understand, though. One day life was normal, and then everyone started acting crazy. We couldn't go out of the house anymore—just Dad would go. Then he went for food and never came back, leaving only me and Mum. We still needed it and Mum wasn't up for leaving me on my own, so she had to take me with her. We would go on food runs together and gather what we could, then head back home.

Food became sparser, and although there were fewer people around, the small numbers that had survived had done so by becoming more brutal. People just took what they wanted, and they would do it by whatever force they found necessary.

Eventually we had to leave our home as there wasn't much food around and the gangs had ransacked all the houses nearby. We moved around a lot, mostly at night. It was scary creeping through the streets in the dark, but Mum said we were less likely to be spotted. It seemed that after nightfall, everyone just partied and was too busy to look out for anyone, whereas through the day, they were all on the hunt.

That was a long time ago now. Mum has been dead for a while. I don't even know what happened to her. One night I went to sleep and when I woke up the next day, she was gone. I know someone must have taken her. She wouldn't have left me, but I don't know why they didn't take or kill me. Mum probably heard them coming and led them away from me. That was the type of person she was—always looking out for her little boy. I wasn't that little anymore, though. I was fifteen when she disappeared, and I was strong for my age. Even though we didn't always have enough to eat, I would always train as hard as I could. I had strong genetics. My father had been a bear of a man and had been in the army for a large part of his life. I suppose that's where I got the whole 'keeping fit' thing from. That and the fact that I always knew that if I was strong, I would have had more chance of protecting my mother.

After she disappeared, I didn't really care about living anymore. So I started to take risks that I'd have never taken before. The first crazy risk I took was approaching a group of four guys that were sitting and having a drink around a bin that they had set on fire. I knew that if they all rushed me at once, they could have killed me, but I had stood and watched them for a while before approaching. I was confident that I could take each of them on their own, and the fact that they seemed to be drunk boosted my confidence. They were a little older than me, but not much. I just walked out from the trees and made a beeline towards them. I was almost on them when one guy jumped up and told me to stay back, quickly followed by his nearest companion, who drew a knife.

"Chill, brother. I'm just looking for heat. Can I join you?" I asked them.

"Who you with? You're too young to be travelling alone," the first guy replied. He was covered in dirt and smelled like shit.

"Ain't with nobody. Travelled with

my mum until she disappeared."

They looked me over and all four of them looked around, scanning the trees I had come from.

"Look guys, I'm on my own. Can I get heat or what?"

After taking a few moments and whispering to each other, they obviously decided I was no threat.

"Fuck it. Take a seat, little man," the smallest one said.

I moved in between two of them and put my hands next to the fire. It felt good to be warm but, on the inside, I was dead. My mother always taught me to be kind when I was younger, but as the world started to change, she taught me about the evil that people could carry inside. She still taught me to be a good man when possible and help others if I could, but I didn't see a whole lot of good growing up, and when she disappeared, I decided that the last good in the world was gone.

The guys were pretty quiet. I think they were sizing me up. They spoke to each other and asked me some questions about my past. They passed a jug between them that contained some foul-smelling liquid but never offered me a drink. I just sat and stared at the fire. I could almost see my mother in the flames. There weren't many waking moments when I didn't think of her.

As time passed by, the guys got drunker. They were getting louder and, while they were trying to keep up a façade of being reasonably friendly, they were hitting me on the back and shoulders harder and smiling at each other. I'm not sure if they were just dumb or if they assumed I was, but it was clear they planned to hurt me. I knew that many people in modern times had turned to cannibalism, even if only on occasion, and I wondered if they had allowed me to join them, thinking that I would be their after drink take-away.

"Gotta take a piss," I told them.

I got up and walked about twenty steps away from the fire. I could hear them begin to whisper and it confirmed my suspicions. I stood for about twenty seconds and walked back to them.

"So, who's first?"

They all looked at each other. I could

tell straight away that they weren't expecting it. I slipped my hunting knife from the back of my jeans and plunged it into the throat of the closest guy. His eyes went white. I'm not sure if in that moment he realised he was dead or if it was just the pain, but he was a goner. Pulling it out quickly, I lunged towards the second guy and stabbed him in the heart. My knife was sharpened every day. Sometimes several times a day. There wasn't a lot to do when you travelled alone, and it was a distraction from my thoughts. The knife withdrew from him relatively easily and I turned to the other two. The closest guy put his hands up in a show of surrender, so I slashed his palms open. The fourth guy took off running. Guy number three pulled his hands back as the blood started to gush. He didn't even try to make a run for it. I smiled at him as I moved closer and quickly slit his throat. I had no intention of torturing these people, but they were bad guys. I could tell, and the world was better off without them. I rummaged through their belongings and found that there wasn't much to take. I did, however, find a few torn pairs of girls' panties, which confirmed my suspicions that they weren't good people. Just as I had thought, good people have no place anymore. When the civilised world ended, it left only room for the animals. My mother was the last good person alive, and I was sure as hell not going to go out like she did. I might have only been fifteen, but I was going to be the hunter.

After that night, I just kept travelling. I had heard rumours over the years of a bar that still functioned after the world ended. They were supposed to have beer on tap, and not the shit people brewed themselves. I knew it was probably bullshit. I had even heard they still had entertainment on each night, and it was like stepping back into the past. Even if it was a myth, I had nothing else to do with my time.

As I travelled, I wondered if I was part of the evil that walked the earth now. My mind went back on forth with it, but I concluded that everyone was either a predator or prey, and I had no intention of being the latter. It was rare that I came across other survivors, but when I did, if they were a largish group, I bypassed them.

If there were four or less, I killed them. A few guys managed to pull their own knives on me, but the element of surprise always gave me an edge and I seemed to be faster than most people, even though my size was still growing.

A few months had passed when I arrived in the city that the mythical bar was supposed to be in. I had probably killed about twenty people by that point, all male. I didn't consider myself a murderer. I was sure that, given the chance, I would have been dinner for some of them or just a bit of entertainment for the others. I could see in some of their eyes the darkness that resided within. I never chased down those who ran away. But they were probably dead now, too. The new world was no place for the weak.

The city had been torn apart and set alight. There wasn't much left of it. I crisscrossed what would have once been the main section, and upon finding nothing, I started to work my way further out. I told myself that if a bar had survived and was still functioning, it stood to reason that it was already run by psychos before things went bad.

Weeks passed by as I travelled. I only wished that there were still cars to travel in, but not many of the roads were driveable anyway. I had almost given up hope and was going to start heading north again when I turned onto a street that was pretty well lit up. Not something you see often, or ever anymore, for that matter. I knew in that moment that I had found the bar. I crossed the road for a better look and there, further down the street, was the bar. It looked like it had been untouched by the world around it. As I walked down the street towards it, I could see the neon lights above the door. It was called Satan's Apocalypse. I couldn't fucking believe it. The myth was real. A fully functioning bar with electricity and who knew what else.

I stood outside the door for a few minutes. I wondered what it would be like inside. I wasn't nervous. I knew that anyone who drank in here must be tough and probably scum, but I was ready to die and was sure I'd take a few of the fuckers with me. I wasn't sure, however, that if I left and walked away that I would ever have another destination to go to. This was it. Something had drawn me here, and I was a fucking predator.

I pushed the door open and walked inside. I stood just inside the door and looked around. It was a fair size and had neon lights everywhere. The place smelled of stale sweat, piss, and smoke. There was music playing from the jukebox and a group of guys standing around the pool table. Mostly everyone looked over at me. I made eye contact with them all. After standing there for twenty to thirty seconds, I walked over to the bar. I had no money and doubted that they would deal in physical cash anyway.

I decided to stand at the bar rather than take a stool. I wanted to be ready for anything that came my way. The bartender was a huge hulk of a man. Not all muscle though. One of those naturally big guys with an even bigger stomach. His head was clean shaven, but he had two little tufts of hair at the front, gelled into horn shapes.

"Help you, boy?" he asked me.

"How do you get a beer in this place?"

"Need some tokens, kid."

I wasn't enjoying his 'boy' or 'kid' chat and I wasn't in the mood for riddles. I wanted to have my first beer at a bar before I would happily go to meet my mother, and that fat fuck was testing my patience.

"You going to make me guess how I get those, or you gonna tell me before I start to get pissed off?"

He smiled widely. "I like that attitude,

sonny boy. You might even have a chance of getting a beer if you keep that up. This bar is all about the entertainment. People come from all over and not many leave, if you know what I'm saying. You want a beer, take someone's tokens. Easy as that."

I turned my back on him and scanned the bar. I was confident that there were no good people in the bar. Certainly no one that I would feel guilty about hurting. Maybe the waitresses. They looked innocent. Maybe not innocent, but not evil. The rest, though, looked like they would rob their best friend. I didn't really care. I had come all this way, and I wanted a beer. I didn't know if I would leave the bar, but I wanted to taste a beer before whatever was going to happen happened. The bar obviously traded in violence, and I was no stranger to that.

Just as I was picking my unsuspecting victim, a tall skinny guy who looked like a rat slapped one of the waitress's asses. She didn't do anything, but she didn't look impressed. I had my man. I contemplated for a minute or two if I should use my knife, then reasoned that I didn't need it. I was over to his side and he was too busy bragging to everyone at the table about what he was going to do to the waitress later. Little did he know, I had crossed the bar in seconds. I could still feel the bartender's eyes following me. I put my hand on my victim's forehead and pulled him backwards, pulling the chair with him. He had already been swinging on the chair and had no chance of catching his balance. When he clattered onto the floor, he looked up at me, eyes wide. He must have noticed I was a young lad and thought he would get the better of me as a smile spread across his rat-like face.

He was wrong.

My foot came down across the middle of his face and obliterated his nose. I could feel the crunch. I didn't stop. I must have stamped on his face eight or nine times, and I could feel bone breaking each time my foot landed. No one at his table moved. Whether it was because I had taken them unaware, because they thought I was a psycho, or because they were so used to the violence and didn't really like Rat Boy anyway, I'm not sure. I knew he was dead before I stopped stomping him, but it was a good release. I could feel some of the anger I carried leaving my body. I bent down and searched his pockets. He had five of the tokens. I didn't know what they were worth, but I slipped them into my pockets. He also had a little metal baton. I took that too. I nodded to the men at the table and made my way back to the bar.

On reaching the bar, the barman had a pint sitting for me already.

"That one is on the house, boy. That was quite a show you put on. I could see you fitting in around here. Be warned, though. Now you gave everyone a show, someone will likely challenge you."

I didn't even answer him. I just picked up my pint and took a swig. I had never tasted beer and I can't say I was all that fond of the taste, but I had earned it and I was going to drink it. As I sipped away, a bell rang.

"What's that for?" I asked the barman.

"Shift change for the waitresses. They work twelve-hour shifts. We never close."

I turned towards the bar patrons and noticed that Rat Boy was gone. Somebody had clearly removed his body. The waitresses were all making their way out of a door and more were spilling in. Just as I watched the new shift filter in, someone appeared at my side.

"So, ye think ye are a ticket, dae ye?"

Without looking, I pulled the metal baton from my pocket and swung it as hard as I could to my right side. As I spun to see the rather large and fat man crumple to the floor, I had already pulled my knife. I slashed it across his eyes and then began to stab him in the chest. Blood squirted everywhere. I knew he wouldn't be getting back up, but I continued to stab him. When I was done, I wiped my knife on the leg of his jeans and slipped it into the back of my jeans. I put the baton back in my pocket, then searched him. This guy had ten of the tokens. He was obviously a bigger asshole than the last, or maybe just a slower drinker.

"He has been here for quite some time. You're lucky you got him before he got you," the bartender said.

"Another pint," I responded.

He slid the pint across the bar. "Cost

you a token this time. As much as you are entertaining, you got the chips from the guys you killed, and you've had your freebie.

I slid two tokens across the bar. I thought it best to keep the barman on my side.

"Is this your place or do you just work here?"

"My place," was all I got in response.

I lifted my pint and turned once again to look over the other patrons. A few were still watching me, but most had gone back to whatever they had been doing before. I considered taking a table, but I liked standing with my back to the bar, where no one could come up behind me. I eyed the waitresses. They all looked a bit worn out, but I couldn't remember the last time I had seen a female.

I was almost finished with my second pint when I saw her… my mother. I rubbed my eyes. It couldn't be, but it was. I walked towards her in a haze. She had her back to me. She had a bucket, and she was tipping the full ashtrays into it. I just stood and waited until she turned. She dropped the bucket, and her hands went to her mouth. I watched her eyes fill with tears.

"What are you doing here?" It was all I could think to ask.

She grabbed my arm and pulled me to the side.

"They took me during the night. They kidnapped me. You have to go. It's not safe here."

I could hear the fear in her voice. To her, I was still her little boy who had to be protected. I couldn't take my eyes off her. She was alive. I never imagined seeing her again, at least not until I was dead.

"Get yourself somewhere safe," I told her as I felt the rage build in my chest. Someone had put their hands on my mother, and they were here.

"What? No… You have to go. You'll get hurt."

I turned my back on her. Something I had never done before. I walked towards the bar at a brisk pace. I was still holding my pint glass, so I threw it straight at the barman. He saw it coming and ducked. I was in the middle of vaulting the bar when he came back up. Both of my feet slammed into his chest and sent him shooting back into the gantry. Bottles smashed all around him as he sunk to the floor. His eyes were wide.

"You can't hurt me. They'll kill you."

I lifted one of the bottles that had fallen on the shelf and brought it down with incredible force over his head. It smashed on the first go, but the neck of the bottle was still in my hand and a large piece of glass was sticking out. I plunged it into his face. I had no idea a man could scream so loud. I have no idea how many times I stabbed him, but I only stopped when someone put their hand on my shoulder. I spun quickly and saw it wasn't my mother, so I head-butted the guy. He flew back into the bar.

Before he righted himself, I pulled my knife from the back of my jeans and slit his throat open. This time, I didn't go wild. I scanned the bar to see who else was coming for me. No one. The rest of the patrons were just standing, watching. When they realised it was over, they started to sit down again. I looked over to my mother. Her jaw was hanging open. I wiped my knife clean and slid it into my jeans. There were two guns under the bar. I could see them while I was looking down at the dead man on the floor. I took both and the extra bullets that were there. I jumped the bar and walked straight over to my mother, keeping one of the guns in my hand, in case anyone got any big ideas. I took her by the arm and walked us both right out of the door. No one followed.

Everything that I've told you happened about a month ago. We are on the move again, looking for good people, if there are any left. My mother doesn't look at me the same anymore. I'm not sure I'm her little boy now. I'm not sure I want to be. It's a bad world we live in and I would do anything to protect her. No one will ever lay a hand on her again. She won't talk about what happened to her, and that's probably for the best. Some nights, I lie awake and wonder if I'm still a good guy. I'm really not sure. It doesn't matter. There are a lot of bad guys out there and if any of them come near us, they will get to see my dark side.

THE PURGE

By Zoey Xolton

Dark, rhythmic chanting fills the night sky, and I feel the oppressive force of our violent spell growing above us. A tangible maelstrom of sickly green power takes form, roiling with barely contained hate.

Dreary Hollow and its fanatical inhabitants are about to welcome their end.

For centuries the Puritans have burned, drowned, and beheaded our kind. The murder of our Coven Mother? The final straw. Our otherworldly cadence reaches a great crescendo, and throwing our heads back—voices raised in righteous rage—the spell is unleashed.

When morning dawns, the streets run red...and Dreary Hollow is ours once more.

First published in *Curses & Cauldrons*, Blood Song Books, 2019

ABOUT THE PUBLISHER

BLACK HARE PRESS is a small, independent publisher based in Melbourne, Australia.

Founded in 2018, our aim has always been to champion emerging authors from all around the globe and offer opportunities for them to participate in speculative fiction and horror short story anthologies.

Connect

Website: *www.blackharepress.com*

Twitter: *@BlackHarePress*

* 9 7 8 0 6 4 5 0 1 3 9 1 7 *